More
Katie Morag
Island Stories

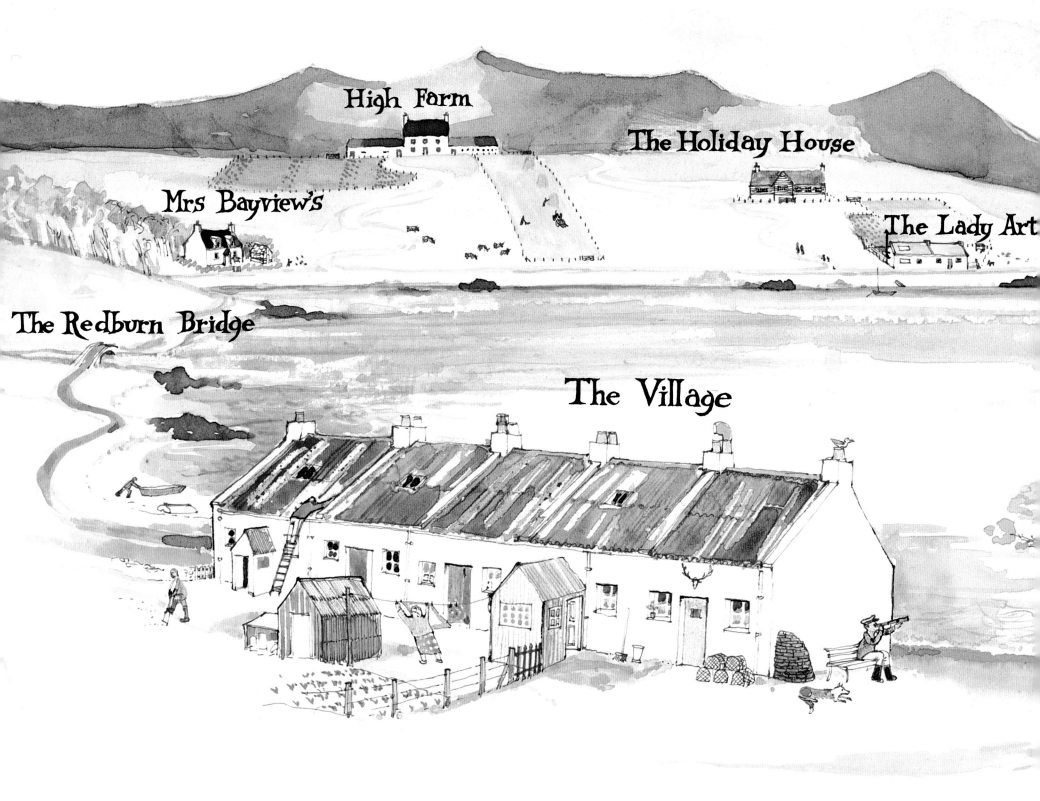

High Farm

The Holiday House

Mrs Bayview's

The Lady Art

The Redburn Bridge

The Village

THE ISLE of STRUAY

Grannie's

The Mainland

ISLE of STRUAY
SHOP & POST OFFICE

OBAN
TIMES
GET
YOUR COPY
HERE

The Jetty

The Shop & Post Office

MORE KATIE MORAG ISLAND STORIES
A RED FOX BOOK 978 1 849 41090 8

First published in Great Britain 2004 by Red Fox,
an imprint of Random House Children's Publishers UK
A Random House Group Company

This Red Fox edition published 2010
Copyright © Mairi Hedderwick, 2004

Originally published as individual editions:
Katie Morag and the New Pier
First published in Great Britain by The Bodley Head in 1993
copyright © Mairi Hedderwick 1993
Katie Morag and the Wedding
First published in Great Britain by The Bodley Head in 1995,
copyright © Mairi Hedderwick 1995
Katie Morag and the Grand Concert
First published in Great Britain by The Bodley Head in 1997,
copyright © Mairi Hedderwick 1997
Katie Morag and the Riddles
First published in Great Britain by The Bodley Head in 2001,
copyright © Mairi Hedderwick 2001

7 9 10 8

Red Fox Books are published by Random House Children's Publishers UK,
61–63 Uxbridge Road, London W5 5SA

www.**randomhousechildrens**.co.uk

Addresses for companies within The Random House Group Limited can be found at:
www.**randomhouse**.co.uk/offices.htm

THE RANDOM HOUSE GROUP Limited Reg. No. 954009

A CIP catalogue record for this book is available from the British Library.

Printed in China

More
Katie Morag
Island Stories

Mairi Hedderwick

RED FOX

KATIE MORAG AND THE NEW PIER

For months workmen had been building a new pier on the Isle of Struay. They were a cheery lot and lived in huts by the shore. They only complained when the weather got too bad to get on with the work; they felt homesick for their families and friends on the mainland.

They looked forward to the day the new pier would be finished. So did the islanders.

MOUSE TRAPS
12 DOZEN

Katie Morag was especially excited about the new pier.

"The boat will be able to come to Struay THREE times a week instead of one," said her father, Mr McColl, the shopkeeper.

Mrs McColl, the postmistress, was delighted. She would have lots more mail deliveries to do.

Post Office

OPEN

For Sale
6 Lobster
Creels

Oban
Times
Buy your
copy
HERE

XMAS
PARTY
FUND

Isle of Struay

R.S.P.B.
Slide
Show
Village Hall
Wed. Evening

ISLE OF STRUAY

"Grandma Mainland will be able to come more often," said Neilly Beag.
"And she will be able to get away quicker," said Grannie Island, who was not very sure about the new pier but saw that it had some advantages.

But for the most part Grannie Island was pessimistic.

"The old ways will be forgotten," she frowned. "The place will get too busy; there will be no more jaunts out in the ferryboat to the big boat in the Bay."

Grannie Island often manned the ferryboat on the days that the ferryman was ill or on holiday. "I'll miss that. And so will you, Katie Morag. And what will the ferryman do for a living?" Katie Morag hadn't thought about all that.

In the village people were saying it was time the old ways changed. They started to paint their windows and gates bright colours and tidy their gardens. Mrs Baxter said she was going to open up a Craft Shop. The Lady Artist, of course, was already making interesting things to sell in it.

On the other side of the Bay Mr MacMaster, the farmer, was very pleased. "I'll be able to send off eggs, milk and cheese to the mainland THREE times a week!"

TOILETS

ISLE of STRUAY
Shop & Post Office

SHOP →

CRAFTS →

TOURIST
FACILIT...

Paintings
for Sale →

"Ach well," sighed the ferryman, "I suppose I'll soon be redundant."

"What does that mean?" asked Katie Morag.

"No longer wanted," replied the ferryman as he and Katie Morag walked along the shore. Katie Morag nearly tripped over a large, blue, neatly coiled rope on the tideline.

"Finders keepers," said the ferryman. "That's the rule of the sea when something is washed up by the tide."

"Oh no – I'll give it to the ferryboat," declared Katie Morag.

"Have you been having chocolate cake again?" asked Mrs McColl crossly, as Katie Morag toyed with her tea that night. She had, but it wasn't the cake that was making Katie Morag sad. She tried to tell Mr and Mrs McColl all about the ferryman but her parents were not listening.

CALENDAR

BISTRO

Isle of Struay shop & P.O.
EXTENSION PLAN

"The pier will be finished by the spring, weather permitting," said Mrs McColl looking at the calendar.

CALENDAR

BISTRO PLANS

Spring came but it did not come alone. It was accompanied by fearsome storms. One especially wet and windy day the foreman on the pier told the men to tie down the equipment and stop work. It was boring sitting in the huts waiting for the wild weather to end, so the workmen visited the islanders, and sat by their cosy fires and told stories about life on the mainland.

Jimmy and George were in the McColls' kitchen when the foreman burst in.
"The huts are floating out to sea!" he shouted.

Everyone rushed to the door and sure enough there was the new pier awash, but not a hut in sight save one that bobbed and bucked in the Bay. The rest had all sunk.

There was something else bobbing in the Bay. It was the ferryboat! Katie Morag could just make out the ferryman throwing a rope over the handle of the hut door. But as Grannie Island steered the ferryboat alongside, a huge wave lifted the rope off the handle and the hut started to drift out to sea again.

"Use my rope!" shouted Katie Morag at the top of her voice.

Grannie Island revved the boat close to the hut again and as she circled round it so went the strong blue rope.

Everyone cheered as the ferryboat towed the hut to the shore.

"What seamanship!" said the workmen. "What a rope!" said the ferryman, smiling at Katie Morag as he stepped out of the boat.

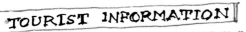

TOURIST INFORMATION

YOU ARE HERE

old pier
new pier
Island of Struay

"You can't sleep in that!" said the islanders as sodden mattresses and broken bits of furniture fell out of the hut door.

"You will just have to stay with us until the new pier is finished."

"Great!" thought Katie Morag. "Mainland stories every night!"

Next morning the storm had subsided and the men went back to work. The foreman said the ferryman could keep the hut for fire wood. He and the men thought it was just fine staying in the islanders' homes – much more comfortable than the huts.

Each workman boasted that his lodgings were the best but everyone had to agree that the ferryman's wife's chocolate cake was quite the most fabbydoo.

It was Easter and the new pier was finally completed. The boat came alongside laden with important people and visitors. And there was Grandma Mainland! The workmen shook hands with the islanders and said they would be back for their holidays. Nearly everyone wanted to book in at the ferryman's house and Katie Morag knew why.

"That's it, then," sighed Grannie Island as hordes of visitors meandered towards the village. "The end of the ferryboat and the old ways."

For Sale

Katie Morag Recipes

Menu

"No, it is not!" said Katie Morag taking her two grandmothers over to the ferryman's house. The hut was transformed: inside, a counter displayed several chocolate cakes and pots of tea. Grandma Mainland was first in the queue.

"After the visitors have had their tea, you and I and Katie Morag can take them out for a jaunt in the ferryboat, Grannie Island," suggested the ferryman.

"And you can tell them all about the old ways," said Katie Morag. Grannie Island smiled. The new pier was not going to be such a bad thing after all.

KATIE MORAG
AND THE WEDDING

Ever since the new pier had been built on the Isle of Struay, Granma Mainland visited regularly.

Katie Morag McColl was delighted to see more of her other grandmother. But most delighted of all the islanders was Neilly Beag. He fancied Granma Mainland and always looked so sad when she went away. Then he would write lots of long letters to her in the city on the mainland and wait impatiently for the mailboat to bring back a reply.

This kept Mrs McColl, the Postmistress, very busy. Everyone on the island said a romance was afoot.

"Maybe even a wedding!" whispered the Ferryman's wife in between serving teas to the visitors.

"Pah! A wedding? I'll believe it when I see it!" muttered Grannie Island when she heard the gossip.

Katie Morag was very excited at the thought of a wedding. It usually meant a big party; it also meant that the two people getting married wanted to live together instead of far apart.

Would Granma Mainland come to live in Neilly Beag's house on the island? That would be lovely! But, oh dear, what if Neilly went to live with Granma Mainland in the far away city?

"If there is a wedding will Neilly Beag be our Grandad?" Katie Morag asked when she and Liam arrived at Grannie Island's, just in time for dinner.

Her Grannie did not answer.

"Wheesht! Go sit at the table!" she frowned instead.

"We've got two grandmothers. Why don't we have two grandfathers?"

"Wheesht! Will you SIT DOWN!" glared Grannie Island.

It was a long time since Katie Morag had seen such a glower in Grannie Island's eye. It was time to stop asking questions.

OLD PHOTOS

As Katie Morag pushed Liam homewards she wondered why Grannie Island was in such a bad mood. It made her feel sad.

When they got to the village Neilly Beag was at his front door. He had a huge pile of stamped addressed envelopes in his arms.

"The invitations for the wedding!" he beamed proudly. "Can you take them to the Post Office, Katie Morag?"

That cheered Katie Morag up no end.

"Can *we* go? Can *we* go?" chorused Katie Morag and Liam when the silver and gold invitation was put on the mantelpiece.

"Of course!" smiled Mr and Mrs McColl. "*Everyone* will be going to the wedding!"

"And the new baby?"

"Of course . . ."

"And the Ferryman and his wife . . . and the Lady Artist . . . and the new teacher?"

"Of course! Of course!" laughed Mr and Mrs McColl.

"And Grannie Island?" asked Katie Morag.

Suddenly everything went very quiet in the McColl kitchen. Grown ups can be very strange thought Katie Morag, sometimes they answer questions and sometimes they do not . . .

That night in bed Katie Morag complained to Liam.

"If we didn't answer when we were asked questions we would be called rude."

"Rood!" agreed Liam.

KATIE MORAG & THE NEW PIER
KATIE MORAG & THE BIG BOY COUSINS
KATIE MORAG & THE TIRESOME TED
KATIE MORAG & THE TWO GRANDMOTHERS
KATIE MORAG DELIVERS THE MAIL

MAY
M T W T F S Sun

"Granma Mainland always answers questions. I am going to write her a letter," declared Katie Morag.

This is what the letter said:

THE SHOP AND POST OFFICE
ISLE OF STRUAY
Proprietors:
Jean and Peter Nicol McColl

Me

May 27

Dear Granma Manelan,
we are looking fowad to yur
wedding. me
Liam
Grannie Eyelan is verry
cross. Can you find her a
Gandad too plese ?
lots of luv and xxxxxx
Katie Morag

PS Liam hops you and Neilly hav
lots of babbies

Peedie Peebles
COLOUR
BOOK

The next few weeks on the island were very busy.

All sorts of parcels and crates came off the boat and were carried up to Neilly's house or to the Village Hall.

Neilly dieted so much Mrs McColl had to get a needle and thread to alter his smart new suit. The Ferryman's wife made a giant of a chocolate cake; she and Mr McColl had to stand on stools to decorate it.

BULK
ICING
SUGAR

COCOA

Katie Morag and Liam made a special present for the bride and groom. The new baby lent ribbons for flags. Liam thought it was Christmas. He kept chanting "Anta Claws! Anta Claws!" and even hung up his stocking. Katie Morag waited for a reply from Granma Mainland.

The day of the wedding drew near.

Granma Mainland and all the relatives and friends were due to arrive on the boat the day before the big event.

Nobody had seen Grannie Island for days.

I'VE FOUND HIM!

All the islanders went to the pier to meet the guests arriving off the boat, but there was *no* sign of Granma Mainland. Neilly Beag was just about to burst into tears when a loud clattering and whirring reverberated around Village Bay.

It was a helicopter and Granma Mainland was right in the front with the white bearded pilot.

"Anta Claws!" yelled Liam.

"It isn't Santa Claus, silly!" cried Katie Morag. *She* knew who it was.

Grandad Island swung Katie Morag up in the air. "Last time I saw you, Katie Morag, you were just a sparkle in your mum and dad's eyes!"

Katie Morag and Liam raced Grandad Island up to the Village Hall to help with the decorations for the wedding party.

Grandad Island asked if Grannie Island was going to the wedding.

"You'd better go and find out for yourself," said Granma Mainland, somewhat sternly.

STRUAY
VILLAGE HALL

KEY AT MRS. BAYVIEW'S
ALWAYS
PLEASE RETURN

FLY

ME

Katie Morag watched Grandad Island set off on the long walk round to Grannie Island's house, on the other side of the bay. She worried that the fierce glare in Grannie Island's eye of late would frighten him away.

The
Wedding
Menu

LOBSTER CLAW SOUP
OR
STUFFED TURNIP
· ~ ·
HAGGIS BURGERS
OR
CARROT STEAKS
· ~ ·
CHIPS
· ~ ·
E CAKE & ICECREAM

Katie Morag need not have worried.

On the day of the wedding nobody's eyes were glaring – everyone's eyes were sparkling, especially the two grandads'. But Grannie Island's and Granma Mainland's were the brightest and sparkliest eyes of all.

Granma Mainland and Neilly Beag were to honeymoon on the neighbouring island of Fuay. There were no people on Fuay, only sheep, and they all belonged to Neilly.

"And all the lambs next spring will be yours, Mrs Beag, my wee Bobby Dazzler!"

Liam was right. Granma Mainland *was* going to have lots of babies to look after.

But Granma Mainland was not going to give up her flat in the city. She and Neilly would commute between Struay, Fuay and the mainland. And Katie Morag could visit whenever she wanted.

It took a lot of persuading to get Grannie Island up in the helicopter.
Grannie Island did not like travelling.

Grandad Island loved travelling and never stayed in one place for long.

"East, West, Home's Best!" insisted Grannie Island, clinging to her
seat like a limpet.

Katie Morag knew then, that Grandad Island would be leaving soon.

"Grandad, when you go travelling can I come too sometimes?"

"Certainly, Katie Morag – anywhere in the world."

Katie Morag was thrilled. She looked forward to visiting Fuay, the city on the mainland and now, anywhere in the world!

But it was good to know that Grannie Island would always be there on the Island of Struay when she got back home.

KATIE MORAG
AND THE GRAND CONCERT

ISLE of STRUAY

Programme

GRAND CONCERT

SVEN & SEAN OLSEN

GERTRUDE ISOBEL

KATIE MORAG McCOLL

BOG COTTON REEL BAND

HEVVIE BEVVIE BAND

NEILLY BEAG

in aid of Struay Music Society

Once in a while on the Isle of Struay there is a Grand Concert.

Everyone who can, practises songs and dances, poems, fiddle and pipe tunes for months in advance.

This concert was going to be extra grand; Katie Morag McColl's uncles Sven and Sean were coming. They were world famous musicians. And they were twins. Everyone practised harder than usual for the special occasion.

Katie Morag asked if she could sing at the Grand Concert.

"Yes! Yes!" answered Mrs McColl impatiently. Liam was missing and the baby had just woken up. "What song?" asked Mr McColl, who was equally preoccupied with stacking shelves.

"I don't know," replied Katie Morag, tearfully.

"Now don't YOU start crying!" shouted Mrs McColl.

"Grannie Island will teach you a song," soothed Mr McColl.

"You'll have to practise every day, remember..." added Mrs McColl.

On the long walk over to Grannie Island's Katie Morag began to wonder if it was such a good idea to perform at the Concert. Suddenly she felt very shy.

"Are you singing at the Grand Concert?" she asked Agnes.

"Oh no!" replied Agnes. "I don't like singing. I like clapping as loud as I can in the audience. I'm going to wear my new dress."

Katie Morag felt even worse.

Grannie Island said she had sung – and danced – with the best in her younger days. "Though nobody would believe that now..." she sighed.

"I do!" said Katie Morag.

Grannie Island got down her fiddle and played 'Ho Ro My Nut Brown Maiden' and 'I Know Where I Am Going' and 'You Cannae Shove Your Granny Off a Bus'. Katie Morag liked the last one best. She soon learned the words which were a bit naughty.

That night in bed Katie Morag fell asleep listening to Grannie Island softly singing Uncle Sven's favourite song; all about a lovely garden and a lady called Maude. Katie Morag wondered if Maude had a pretty new dress.

THE
SONG OF THE
GRANDMOTHERS

YOU CAN SHOVE YOUR <u>OTHER</u> GRANNY OFF A BUS,
YOU CAN SHOVE YOUR OTHER GRANNY OFF A BUS,
YOU CAN SHOVE YOUR OTHER GRANNY,
FOR SHE'S YOUR DADDY'S MAMMY!
YOU CAN SHOVE YOUR <u>OTHER</u> GRANNY OFF A BUS!

When Uncle Sven and Uncle Sean arrived Katie Morag could not work out which uncle was which. They were absolutely identical.

"Hello, Katie Morag!" smiled Sven.

"Hiya, Matie Korag!" smiled Sean.

They had brought lots of presents and an extra one for Katie Morag from Granma Mainland who lived in the faraway city.

A PRESENT from AUSTRALIA

To: Katie Morag McColl
From: Granma Mainland

Inside the box was the most beautiful dress that Katie Morag had ever seen.
"Come and have some parsnip soup after your long journey!"
called Mrs McColl. Sven had two helpings, Sean had three.
"Delicious!" said Sven.
"Fabbydoo!" said Sean.

After supper Uncle Sven and Uncle Sean said they would like to practise for the concert. Katie Morag said she would too and was allowed to stand on the table to sing her song.

When it got to the bit, "You can shove your OTHER granny off a bus" everyone laughed.

But Katie Morag knew she wouldn't ever do such a thing to either of her grandmothers. It was just a joke. She loved them both too much.

"Well done!" cheered Uncle Sven.

"Right Bobby Dazzling!" cheered Uncle Sean.

It was going to be a WONDERFUL concert, thought Katie Morag.

: Katie Morag McColl
: Granma Mainland

"Goodnight, sleep well," yawned Uncle Sven when it was time for bed.

"Tattie bye, peepers sleepers," yawned Uncle Sean.

"Where is Liam!" worried Mrs McColl.

Liam was nowhere to be seen.

He was not behind the couch, nor under the table; he was not in the loo nor inside the biscuit cupboard; he was not in his bed.

"The door!" cried Katie Morag. It was wide open...

ISLE of STRUAY   YOU ARE HERE

Everyone went shouting out into the night, waving torches.

"Liam! Liam! Where are you? Come here! Come here!"

Uncle Sven shouted the loudest and longest.

Mrs McColl was quite distraught. "He's in the sea!" she screamed.

All the lights and shouting woke Liam up.

Liam nearly wasn't allowed to go to the Concert after causing so much trouble. Mrs McColl relented at the last minute.

Katie Morag peeped through the curtains. She was so excited! The dress fitted perfectly and look! Granma Mainland had caught the second boat. There she was sitting in the front row looking so pretty. Liam was beside her, holding her hand.

Everything was perfect.

And then Katie Morag saw Agnes. She was also sitting in the front row. And she was wearing the EXACT SAME DRESS...

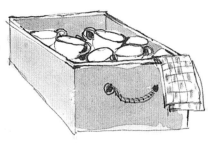

No one was ever, ever as miserable as Katie Morag was at that precise moment. She ran off backstage, big tears filling her eyes.

"I'm not singing!" she wailed at Grannie Island.

And there was Uncle Sven with big tears in his eyes, too. "I've lost my voice," he croaked.

Grannie Island tried to comfort them both, her own eyes glistening. The Concert was a disaster before it had even started.

It was a terrible thing to see grown ups with tears in their eyes, thought Katie Morag, as she rubbed her own dry.

GRAND CONCERT
Artistes

SVEN & SEAN DUO

KATIE MORAG SOLO

HEVVIE BEVVIE BAND

GERTRUDE ISOBEL
FIDDLE

BOG COTTON REEL BAND

NEILLY BEAG
RECITATION

Come into the Garden, Maude

"Come on, Uncle Sean. I'll sing Uncle Sven's song for him."

Grannie Island gave Sven a hankie and then her fiddle. "You don't need a voice for this," she encouraged, pushing him onto the stage behind Katie Morag and Uncle Sean.

The trio gave the performance of their lives. The audience went wild. Agnes clapped until her hands were sore.

The Grand Concert was off to a very grand start!

Katie Morag did not mind not singing the Granny song. It would not be so very funny with the two grandmothers listening, would it?

At the end of the night there was a party in the Village Hall. All the islanders wanted Sven and Sean's autographs. "Do you know which is Sven and which is Sean?" they whispered.

Katie Morag and Agnes had their own party up on the stage. They had so enjoyed being twins they decided to wear the same clothes one day a week from now on – and confuse everybody.

Do you know which one is Katie Morag and which is Agnes?

"I do!" said Uncle Sven.

And Uncle Sean said, "Fabbydoolidoozie, so do I!"

KATIE MORAG AND THE RIDDLES

"I hate school!" thought Katie Morag.

The Big Boy Cousins were making an oil rig and Agnes was allowed to help. The teacher had asked Katie Morag for the second day running to show the wee ones how to thread beads.

"Baby stuff!" she muttered. "Everyone else gets better things to do than me!" Katie Morag was very peeved.

But Liam was delighted that his big sister had come to help.

WAKEY!
WAKEY!

"I have got a sore tummy," said Katie Morag next morning when the family was at breakfast.

"Eat up your porridge and it will go away," said her mother, Mrs McColl. "Hurry up or you'll be late for school. You haven't even got your clothes on yet! HURRY UP!"

"Is it really sore?" asked her father, Mr McColl.

"REALLY sore," wailed Katie Morag.

STRUAY P.S.

Mr McColl tucked Katie Morag up in her parents' bed. It was lovely snuggling down under the big duvet and hearing Liam going off to school with Mrs McColl and the baby in the pushchair. She listened to Mr Mc Coll humming to himself as he tidied the kitchen before going downstairs to open up the Shop and Post Office.

It was so peaceful and quiet being left alone.

Katie Morag soon got bored, however. She got out of bed, her sore tummy quite gone, and put on her mother's best shoes and lipstick and perfume. Mrs McColl's nightie was like a ball gown; her necklace so pretty.

But as Katie Morag pirouetted round the room the thread of Mrs McColl's favourite necklace broke.

In a panic, Katie Morag collected the scattered beads.
She ran to her room and hid them in her secret hiding place.
She would get the special needle and bead thread from school.
She was desperate to go to school now.

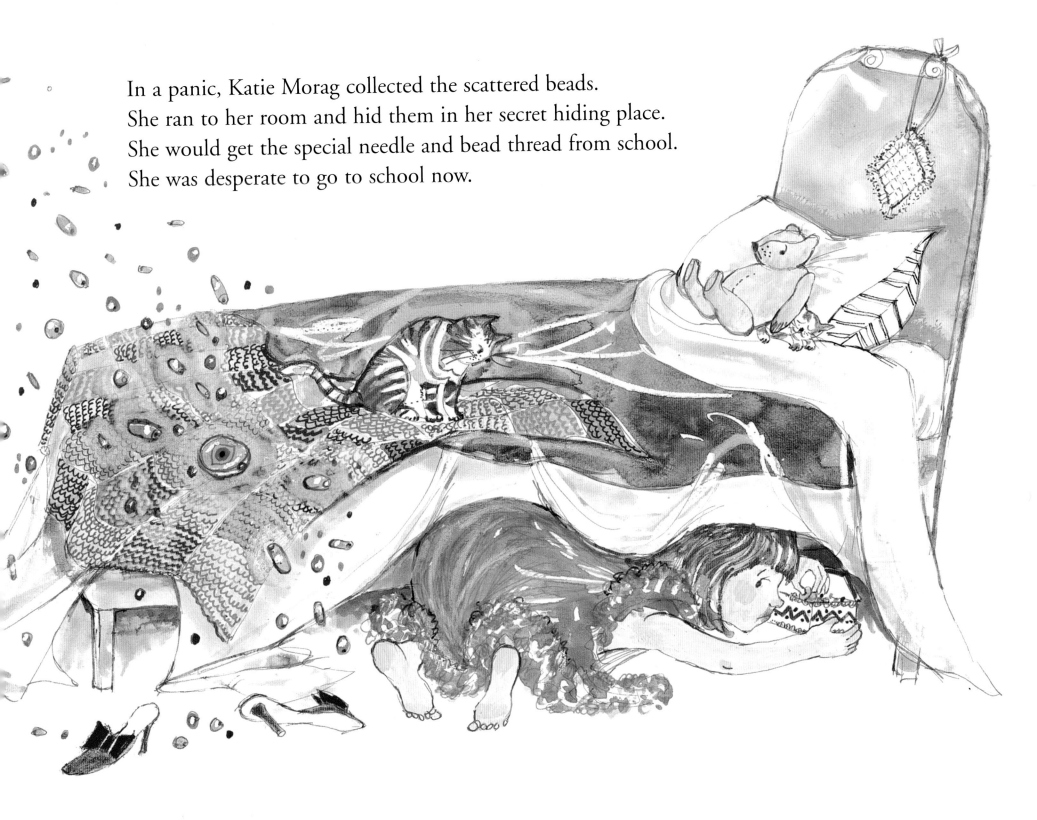

Next day the Teacher said that Jamie could help the wee ones. "PLEASE let me," Katie Morag pleaded. "I LOVE helping the wee ones!"

"Really?" asked the Teacher, in amazement.

"Give me the needle and thread!" Katie Morag whispered to her little brother.

But Liam said, in a loud voice, "Go away, Katie Morag! I can do it myself!"

CRAP

"You give them to ME!" screeched Katie Morag.
"Katie Morag!" frowned the Teacher. "Go back to your seat!"

Things got worse for Katie Morag. Because she was so miserable deep down inside she was horrible now to the Big Boy Cousins and Agnes. So they were horrible to her.

After lunch there was a terrible squabble in the playground.

"Katie Morag started it!" accused the Big Boy Cousins.

"You big ones should know how to behave better!" said the Teacher, exasperated.
"For your homework I want you all to work together to find the answers to
these riddles by Monday."

"I don't understand any of this," growled Hector, the biggest Big Boy Cousin, when he tried to make sense of the riddles. "Listen. It's glaikit blethers:

No. 1: *The land was white,*
The seed was black;
It will take a good scholar
To riddle me that.

No. 2: *As round as an apple,*
As deep as a pail;
It never cries out,
Till it's caught by its tail.

No. 3: *Four stiff-standers,*
Four dilly-danders,
Two lookers,
Two crookers,
And a wig wag.

No 4: *A wee, wee man*
In a dark red coat;
A staff in my hand,
And a stone in my throat.
Who am I?"

"This is all your fault, Katie Morag!" The Cousins and Agnes glowered at her.

"I'll get the answers," mumbled Katie Morag, miserably, hoping they would leave her alone. And they did, running off with whoops of joy. "See you Monday morning then, with all the answers, Katie Morag!"

Katie Morag was grateful when Liam took her hand on the slow journey home.

WELCOME
TO
TRUAY SCHOOL

The next day, Katie Morag went to see Grannie Island.

"So, Miss Mopus, what is the long face for?" Grannie Island asked.
Katie Morag told Grannie Island her troubles.
But she said nothing about the necklace.

"Well, you have come to the right place for the first riddle," said Grannie Island.

> *The land was white,*
> *The seed was black;*
> *It will take a good scholar*
> *To riddle me that.*

"Look at the book on my knee!" nudged Grannie Island.
Katie Morag looked hard; the white pages were like square fields and the letters like black seeds planted in rows!

"Books don't always have answers," mused Grannie Island. "Sometimes people know answers better…"

As round as an apple, As deep as a pail; It never cries out, Till it's caught by its tail.

No. 2

Four stiff-standers, Four dilly-danders, Two lookers, Two crookers, And a wig wag.

No. 3

Katie Morag told everyone she met on the way home all about the riddles.

The Lady Artist was polishing her big doorbell. "Stop pulling its tail, silly old goat! What a clanging, Katie Morag!"

Mr McMaster was herding Dilly, the cow, into the byre for milking. "Grab the pail, Katie Morag, and you can help!"

A wee wee man, In a dark red coat; A staff in my hand, and a stone in my throat. Who am I?

No. 4

Mrs Bayview was in her orchard picking dark red cherries. "Careful you don't swallow a stone, Katie Morag!"

Katie Morag had found the answers to all the riddles! Have you?

Katie Morag was first at school on Monday morning. The Big Boy Cousins and Agnes were worried that she did not have all the answers to the riddles.

Katie Morag handed over the answers with a big grin.

"Well done!" smiled the Teacher. "I am glad you worked together so well. I hope that is the end of all the squabbling?"

"Oh, yes!" replied The Big Boy Cousins and Agnes, relieved. "We think Katie Morag is great. She worked the hardest of all!"

At the end of the day, Katie Morag asked if she could borrow the special needle and thread for making necklaces. "Of course!" smiled the Teacher. Once Katie Morag got Mrs McColl's necklace mended, all her troubles would be over.

Katie Morag made Liam run all the way home. She raced up to her bedroom but Mrs McColl's beads were not in the hiding place. They were gone!

Oh dear, what if her mother had found them? Would she think Katie Morag had stolen them? Oh dear, oh dearie me! Everything was awful again. Mrs McColl often wore that necklace in the evenings…

But someone had already mended Mrs McColl's necklace!

ISLE of STRUAY

Mrs McColl asked Liam how he had got on at school. "I threaded the beads without any help from Katie Morag," Liam said proudly.

"I'm glad that sore tummy of yours has gone away, Katie Morag," winked Mr McColl.

"So am I," laughed Katie Morag. "I'm looking forward to school tomorrow."
She was feeling ever so much better.

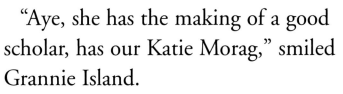

"Aye, she has the making of a good scholar, has our Katie Morag," smiled Grannie Island.
And there were the Big Boy Cousins and Agnes at the door waiting to play.

TEAS

Join Katie Morag on more adventures!